ALPHABETICA
odes to the alphabet

diana spieker • krista skehan

for james because of t

thank you mom for
encouraging my playful spirit &
love to my husband, dan for
keeping it alive

Text Copyright © 2007 by Diana Spieker

Illustrations & Design Copyright © 2007 by Krista Skehan

Published in 2007 by Personify Press, LLC, San Francisco

ISBN 978-0-9797491-0-0   Printed in Singapore

For more information, please visit www.personifypress.us

In these pages try to find
pictures mixed along with rhyme.
Everyone can play this game,
for every image has a name -
beginning with the letter A
and on to Z – hip hip hooray!

ACROBATS

Trapeze artists tumbling
every appendage falling
Now catching, then fumbling
Acrobats flipping-flopping
Inverted bodies somersaulting
aerial flex of limber gymnastics
Twirling and twisting
to reaches fantastic

HIP HIP HOORAY
for ACROBATS!

BUBBLES

fizzy dazzling frothing
a bubbly boisterous sky parade
shimmering swimming then POPPING
a bubbling whimsical escapade
bubbles floating then exploding
bath time soap, so foamy, sudsy
bubbles, bubbles fun and lovely

HIP HIP HOORAY FOR BUBBLES!

CARNIVALS

come one come all to the county fair
confections from the concessionaire
I'm the cavalier on the carousel

save me a chair on the Ferris wheel
oh me oh my, roller coasters, cotton candy
ring toss — first prize! everybody cheering, clapping...

HIP-HIP HOORAY

FOR CARNIVALS!

DOGS

THEY WOOF AND THEY JUMP AND THEY WAG AND THEY DIG

THEY PANT WHEN IT'S HOT WHETHER DAINTY OR BIG

THEY'LL DO SILLY TRICKS IF YOU DANGLE A TREAT

THEY DROOL OVER FOOD – ESPECIALLY MEAT!

YIPPY DOGS. HOWLING DOGS. BIG BARKING HAPPY DOGS

HIP HIP HOORAY FOR DOGS!

EARTH

EXQUISITE LIFE-GIVING, LIVING PLANET
SPINNING IN CIRCLES, EMBRACED BY THE SUN,
YOUR ELEGANCE HAS US COMPLETELY ENCHANTED
YOUR ELEMENTS PRECIOUS: AIR, FIRE, WATER, & MUD
BLESS ME BLUE, BLESS ME GREEN – EVERY COLOR IN BETWEEN
WHAT EXCITING EDUCATION – THIS EARTHLY EXPLORATION
WE DISCOVER AS WE SAVE AND CARE, YOU GIVE BACK BEYOND COMPARE

HIP HIP HOORAY FOR THE EARTH!

fire

flaming, gilded dancer

in an orange flaring dress

flash and flicker candle-prancer

glowing kindle incandesce

shining you shimmer, blazing you gleam

waltzing with darkness to radiate warmth;

fiery glimmer you splendor of sheen

amazed by your light, we watch you perform

hip hip hooray for fire!

Grasshoppers

hippity hoppity flying dreamer

grass-colored, gamboling creature

green hopper so glorious

giant cricket notorious

leap and glide

leap and glide and touch the sky

HIP HOP HOORAY FOR

Grasshoppers

HEARTBEAT

HEARTBEAT, HEARTBEAT, LITTLE DRUMMER
SOUNDING THUNDER
IN MY RIBS I FEEL YOU FLUTTER
HEARTBEAT RACING WHEN I RUN
HEARTBEAT PACING THUMP THUMP THUMP
MEASURED METER, PITTER PATTER
PULSING RHYTHM, MY HEART CHATTERS

HIP HIP HOORAY FOR MY HEARTBEAT!

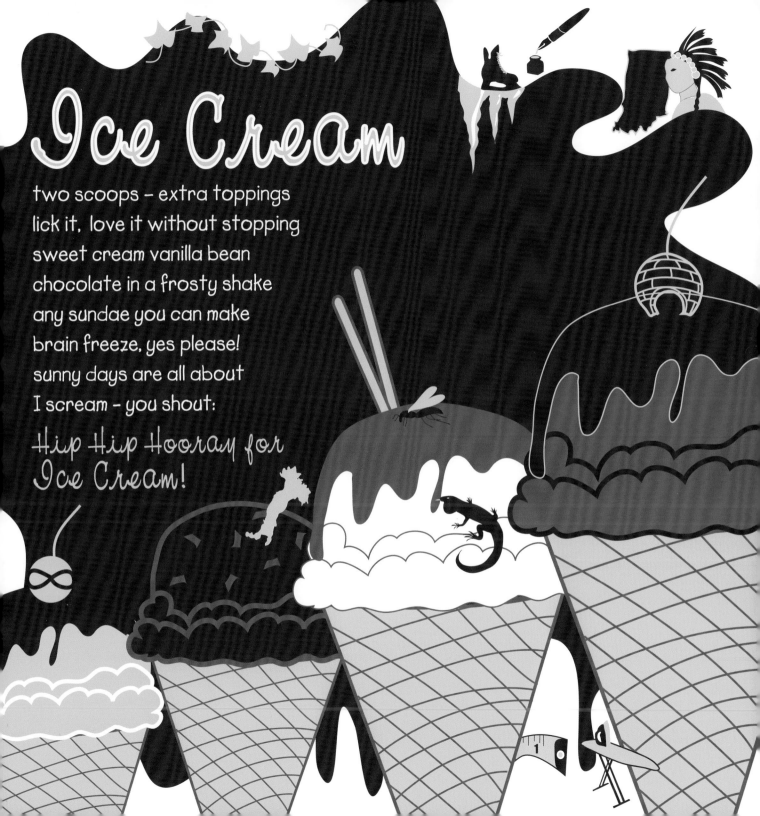

Ice Cream

two scoops – extra toppings
lick it, love it without stopping
sweet cream vanilla bean
chocolate in a frosty shake
any sundae you can make
brain freeze, yes please!
sunny days are all about
I scream – you shout:

Hip Hip Hooray for
Ice Cream!

JUICE

dribble of purplish grapish sweet
orange – oh joy! a juice jubilee
slurp it up, in a cup
through a straw, drink it raw
summer fruit
makes tangy juice
happy apple
ever after
Hip Hip Hooray for JUICE!

kites

kites flying, kites rising
reaching up to kiss the sky
running, then throwing
a gust in the wings
lifting then swerving
unraveling strings
the colors are blending
with sky never ending

hip hip hooray for kites!

Lady Bugs

lady bug little hug
she thinks I am her tree
lovely painted dainty one
you are safe with me
fly away lady bug
to make my wish come true
come again lady bug
some other afternoon

Hip Hip Hooray for Lady Bugs!

MOON

sliver of silver
HEY DIDDLE DIDDLE
night light
MOON RISE
full moon howl tonight
SWEET SLEEP
moon beams
MELTING INTO DREAMS

Hip Hip Hooray for the MOON!

Noise

music makers, band players, banging on a drum

hand clap, finger tap

everybody sing along

shouting, screeching, howling, ringing

ear awakening

clarion clamor

trumpeting, tinkling

bellowing jammer

Hip Hip Hooray for

Noise!

NEWS

NORTH

Ocean

BIG FOAMY CRASHING WAVES

WIDE BRIMMING SEA

OCEAN SPRAYS, OCEAN BREEZE

EBB AND FLUX OF ENERGY

BRINY SAND, SALTY AIR

DOLPHINS, OYSTERS, FISH, & WHALES

SAILING THE OCEAN, CRUISING THE TIDES

INTO THE DEEP BLUE AQUATIC ALIVE

Hip Hip Hooray FOR THE Ocean!

Puddles

splishy-splashy, getting drenched

puddle-jumping, sopping wet

bouncing, skipping, playing hopscotch

rainy games in wet galoshes

water waits in shallow pools

muddy magic & kersploosh!

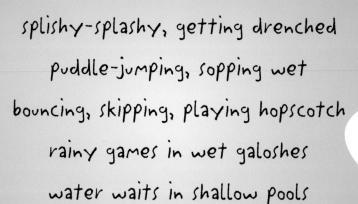

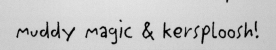

Hip Hip Hooray for

Puddles!

"Quack!"

says the mama duck
her duckling quacks back
the drake might quack
if he wants a little snack
you can spot a duck in flight
by the quantity of quacking
also quite a bit of flapping
never quitting to alight

Quick Quick Hooray
for Quack!

ROCKETS

10...9...8...
ROCKETS RACE
LAUNCHING INTO OUTER SPACE

7...6...
ROCKETSHIP
NAVIGATING CONSTELLATIONS
PLANETARY EXPLORATION

5...4...
ROCKETS SOAR
ZOOMING THROUGH THE GALAXY
REACHING ORBIT - FINALLY

3...2...1...
Blast Off!

Hip Hip Hooray for
ROCKETS!

SUMMER

THE SEASON OF
SPRINKLERS & HOTDOGS
ICE CREAM & BACKYARDS
FIREFLIES, BIKE RIDES
TRIPS TO THE SEA-SIDE
SWIMMING POOLS – NO SCHOOL!
LONG DAYS AND CLEAR SKIES
BLUE IN MY WIDE EYES

HIP HIP HOORAY FOR
SUMMER!

TREES

oh! timber in towers
ancient and powerful
the treasure of green
in each delicate leaf

oh! generous titan
terrestrial giant
the fan of your canopy
framing the sky for me

oh! tangle of branches
a tree house, a swing
from one tiny seed
possibility springs

hip hip hooray for
TREES!

UKULELE

playful charm

beach guitar   bouncing sounding

UKULELE

singing strings   island music   hula dreams

hip hip hooray
for the
UKULELE!

VOLCANOS

volcanos are violent
and furious beasts
they spew out hot lava
erupting from peaks
in rivers and streams
it flows down the mountain
a burp in the earth
with a red molten fountain

hip hip hooray for

VOLCANOS!

Wind

cool breath of the air
a swirl of unseen
blustery rustle
soft whistling breeze

gusty surge in the sky
cloudy vaporous blast
a gale whirling wild
weather's frolicking draft

hip hip hooray for the Wind!

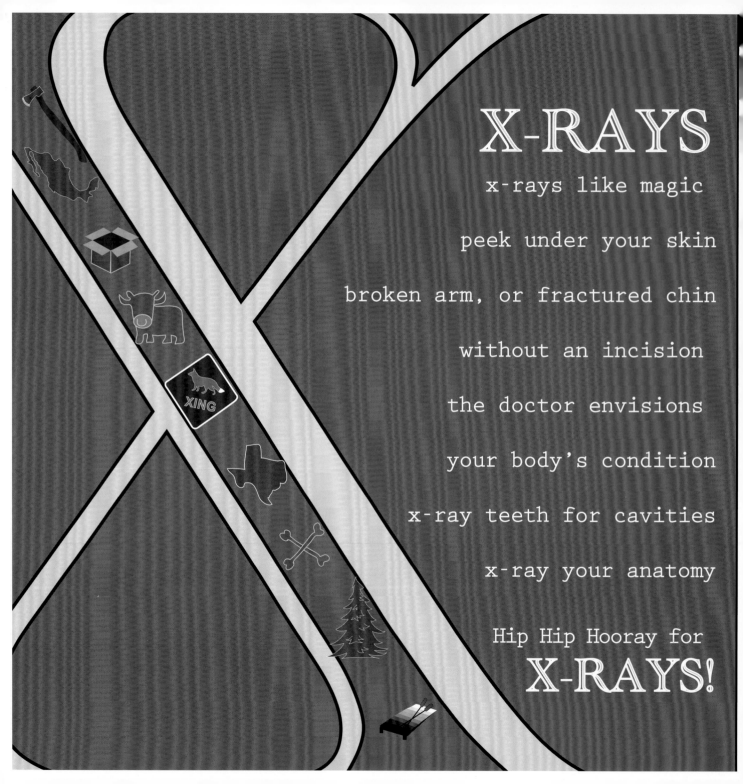

X-RAYS

x-rays like magic

peek under your skin

broken arm, or fractured chin

without an incision

the doctor envisions

your body's condition

x-ray teeth for cavities

x-ray your anatomy

Hip Hip Hooray for
X-RAYS!

you

you good thing, you best of all

you wow and amaze me

I love you like crazy

you miracle in just my size

you sun-shiny

favorite of mine

you squeeze and hug

you baby-love

all my forever

wishes come true

hip hip hooray for

you!

Zippers

ZAP! zing!

zooM

this zipper zooms up

that zipper zings down

a slippery slider

a zipping collision

when zipping I'm loving

the sound of the buzzing

a zippity song

with my zipping precision

Zip Zip Hooray for Zippers!

Zoo Animals

Alligator

Patricia Whitehouse

Heinemann Library
Chicago, Illinois

© 2003 Reed Educational & Professional Publishing
Published by Heinemann Library,
an imprint of Reed Educational & Professional Publishing,
Chicago, Illinois

Customer Service 888-454-2279
Visit our website at www.heinemannlibrary.com

Designed by Sue Emerson, Heinemann Library
Printed and bound in the United States by Lake Book Manufacturing, Inc.

07 06 05 04 03
10 9 8 7 6 5 4 3 2 1

Library of Congress Cataloging-in-Publication Data
Whitehouse, Patricia, 1958-
    Alligator / Patricia Whitehouse.
        p. cm. — (Zoo animals)
Includes index.
Summary: An introduction to alligators, including their size, diet and everyday life style, which highlights differences between those in the wild and those living in a zoo habitat.
    ISBN: 1-58810-903-8 (HC), 1-40340-642-1 (Pbk.)
    1. Alligators—Juvenile literature. [1. Alligators. 2. Zoo animals.] I. Title.
    QL666.C925 W47 2002
    597.98—dc21

2001006870

Acknowledgments
The author and publishers are grateful to the following for permission to reproduce copyright material:
Title page, p. 4 Ken Lucas/Visuals Unlimited; p. 5 Jo Prater/Visuals Unlimited; pp. 6, 11, 22, 24 Chicago Zoological Society/The Brookfield Zoo; p. 7T M. C. Chamberlain/DRK Photo; p. 7B Tom & Pat Leeson/DRK Photo; p. 8 Joe McDonald/Visuals Unlimited; p. 9 Marty Cordano/DRK Photo; p. 10 David Northcott/DRK Photo; p. 12 Arthur Morris/Visuals Unlimited; p. 13 Raymond Gehman/Corbis; p. 14 Doug Perrine/DRK Photo; p. 15 Betsy Strasser/Visuals Unlimited; p. 16 Tom & Pat Leeson/Photo Researchers, Inc.; p. 17 Peter Scoones/BBC Natural History Unit; p. 18 Gerard Fuehrer/DRK Photo; p. 19 Rick Poley/Visuals Unlimited; p. 20 John Cancalosi/Peter Arnold, Inc.; p. 21 Jim Brandenburg/Minden Pictures; p. 23 (row 1, L-R) M. C. Chamberlain/DRK Photo, T. Clutter/Photo Researchers, Inc., Ken Lucas/Visuals Unlimited; p. 23 (row 2, L-R) Sue Emerson/Heinemann Library, Lawrence M. Sawyer/PhotoDisc, Ken Lucas/Visuals Unlimited; p. 23 (row 3, L-R) Chicago Zoological Society/The Brookfield Zoo, W. Bertsch/Bruce Coleman Inc., Doug Perrine/DRK Photo; back cover (L-R) Joe McDonald/Visuals Unlimited, Ken Lucas/Visuals Unlimited

Cover photograph by C. C. Lockwood/Visuals Unlimited
Photo research by Bill Broyles

Every effort has been made to contact copyright holders of any material reproduced in this book.
Any omissions will be rectified in subsequent printings if notice is given to the publisher.

Special thanks to our advisory panel for their help in the preparation of this book:

Eileen Day, Preschool Teacher
Chicago, IL

Ellen Dolmetsch,
Library Media Specialist
Wilmington, DE

Kathleen Gilbert,
Teacher
Round Rock, TX

Sandra Gilbert,
Library Media Specialist
Houston, TX

Angela Leeper,
Educational Consultant
North Carolina Department
of Public Instruction
Raleigh, NC

Pam McDonald, Reading Teacher
Winter Springs, FL

Melinda Murphy,
Library Media Specialist
Houston, TX

We would also like to thank Lee Haines, Assistant Director of Marketing and Public Relations at the Brookfield Zoo in Brookfield, Illinois, for his review of this book.

Some words are shown in bold, **like this.**
You can find them in the picture glossary on page 23.

Contents

What Are Alligators?

scales

Alligators are **reptiles**.

Reptiles have **scales** on their bodies.

Alligators might be hard to see in the wild.

But you can see them at the zoo.

What Do Alligators Look Like?

Alligators have long tails and short legs.

They are dark gray or dark green.

alligator

crocodile

Alligators and **crocodiles** look almost the same.

But most of an alligator's teeth don't show.

What Do Baby Alligators Look Like?

A baby alligator looks like its parents, but it is smaller.

Baby alligators are black with yellow stripes.

Baby alligators come out of eggs.

A new baby alligator can fit in your hand.

Where Do Alligators Live?

In the wild, alligators live in **swamps**.

They live where it is warm all year.

In zoos, alligators live in **enclosures.**

The enclosures are filled with plants and water.

What Do Alligators Eat?

In the wild, alligators eat fish and frogs.

They also eat small animals that come near the water.

At the zoo, alligators eat chicken.

They eat only a few times a week.

What Do Alligators Do All Day?

snout

Alligators spend a lot of time floating in the water.

Their **snouts** stick out so they can breathe.

14

On land, alligators lie in the sun.

When they get too hot, they go in the water.

When Do Alligators Sleep?

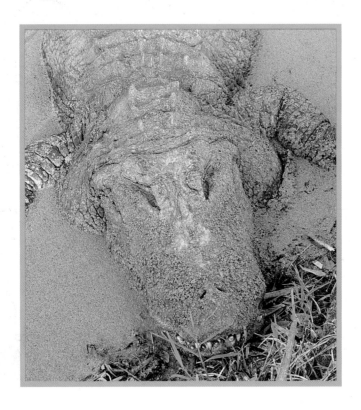

Alligators are **nocturnal**.

They sleep during the day.

In the wild, alligators hunt for food at night.

What Sounds Do Alligators Make?

Alligators roar and growl.

They hiss at animals passing by.

Mother alligators grunt to
their babies.

The baby alligators grunt back.

How Are Alligators Special?

There were alligators when **dinosaurs** were alive.

Scientists know this because of **fossils** they find.

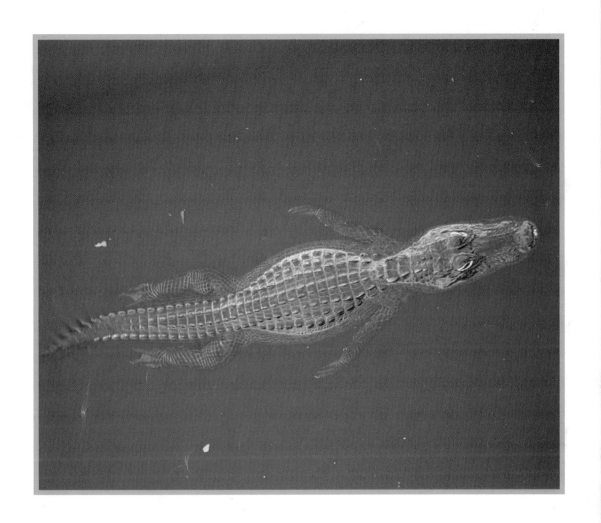

Alligators have not changed much since dinosaur times.

Alligators still look almost the same today.

Quiz

Do you remember what these alligator parts are called?

Look for the answers on page 24.

?   ?   ?

Picture Glossary

crocodile
page 7

fossil
page 20

scales
page 4

dinosaur
pages 20, 21

nocturnal
page 16

snout
page 14

enclosure
page 11

reptile
page 4

swamp
page 10

Note to Parents and Teachers

Reading for information is an important part of a child's literacy development. Learning begins with a question about something. Help children think of themselves as investigators and researchers by encouraging their questions about the world around them. In this book, the animal is identified as a reptile. A reptile is an animal that has dry, usually scaly skin and that is cold-blooded. The symbol for reptile in the picture glossary is an iguana. Point out to children that many other animals besides alligators and iguanas are reptiles, including lizards, snakes, and turtles.

Index

Answers to quiz on page 22

snout   scales   tail

24